MONKEY, WHERE ARE YOU?

David Martin ILLUSTRATED Scott Nash

Introduction

Before your child starts reading, read this story description. Then look through the book together and talk about the pictures.

This story is called *Monkey, Where Are You?* It's about all the places Monkey hides from Mom.

Monkey hides in the box.

"Monkey, where are you?"

Monkey hides in the sink.

"Monkey, where are you?"

Monkey hides in the drawer.

"Monkey, where are you?"

Monkey hides in the garbage.

"I found you," says Mom.